Every new generation of children is enthralled by the famous stories in our Well-loved Tales series. Younger ones love to have the story read to them. Older children will enjoy the exciting stories in an easy-to-read text.

WELL-LOVED TALES

The Wolf and the Seven Little Kids

retold for easy reading
by VERA SOUTHGATE MA B Com
illustrated by ROBERT AYTON

Ladybird Books Loughborough

Once upon a time there was a goat who had seven little kids. She loved them all dearly. Her only fear was that one day the wolf might catch them. One day the mother goat had to go into the forest to look for food. Before she went, she called her seven little kids to her.

"Dear children," she said, "while I am out, take care that the wolf does not come near you. Keep the door locked. If he gets in, he will eat every one of you. He may disguise himself but you will know him by his rough voice and black feet."

The kids replied, "Dear mother, do not worry; we'll take good care of ourselves." So the mother goat went off into the forest, leaving her kids at home.

It was not long before there was a knock on the door. Someone called out, "Open the door for your mother, dear children. She has brought something back for each of you."

But the little kids knew that such a rough voice could not be their mother's. "We won't open the door," they cried. "You are not our mother. She has a gentle voice but yours is rough. You are the wolf!"

Then the wolf went to a shop and bought himself a lump of chalk. He ate the whole of it, hoping to make his voice soft. He then returned to the house and knocked on the door.

"Open the door for your mother, dear children. She has brought something back for each of you," said the wolf in a gentle voice.

As the wolf spoke he put his black paws on the window-sill.

The kids heard the soft voice and thought, at first, that it was their mother's. Then they saw the black paws and cried, "We won't open the door. You are not our mother. She has not got black feet. You are the wolf!"

At these words, the wolf ran to the baker. "I have hurt my foot," he said. "Rub some dough on it for me."

The baker was afraid of the wolf and so he did as he was told.

Next the wolf ran to the miller. "Sprinkle some flour over my foot for me," he said.

The miller thought to himself, "The wolf wants to deceive someone," so he refused. At that the wolf said, "If you do not do as I tell you, I shall eat you." Then the miller was afraid and he sprinkled flour over the wolf's foot.

For the third time the wolf returned to the goats' house and knocked on the door. "Open the door, dear children, for your mother," he said. "She has brought something back for each of you."

The kids heard the gentle voice but they were still careful. "First show us your paws," they cried, "so that we may know if you are our dear mother."

The wolf put his paw on the window-sill. When the kids saw the white paw they thought that it was truly their mother.

They opened the door wide and *there stood the wolf!*

The kids were terrified and ran to hide themselves.

One ran under the table, the second jumped into bed, the third into the stove, the fourth into the kitchen, the fifth into the cupboard, the sixth under the washing-bowl and the seventh into the clock-case.

It did not take the wolf long to find them and, one after the other, he swallowed them as quickly as possible. The youngest kid, who was hidden in the clock-case, was the only one the wolf did not find.

After swallowing six kids the wolf felt sleepy. He went out into the meadow, lay down under a tree and was soon sound asleep.

Soon afterwards the mother goat came home from the forest. What a sight met her eyes!

The door of the house stood wide open. The tables and chairs had been overturned. The washing-bowl had been broken to pieces. The pillows and bed-clothes had been pulled off the beds.

The mother goat searched for her seven children, but nowhere could she find them.

Then, in despair, she called her kids by their names, one by one. Not one answered until at last she called the name of the seventh kid. When she had called its name, a little voice replied, "Dear mother, I am in the clock-case."

Overjoyed, she took her little kid out of the clock-case. It told her how the wolf had eaten the other six kids. When the sad tale was told, the mother goat and the seventh little kid wept together.

After a while, the poor mother goat, followed by her one little kid, wandered sadly outside into the meadow. There, under a tree, lay the wolf, sound asleep. He was snoring so loudly that the branches of the tree above him shook.

The mother goat walked round the sleeping wolf and saw his huge, swollen stomach. When she looked more closely, she thought that something was moving and struggling inside his stomach.

"Goodness me!" she cried. "Is it possible that my little kids, whom he swallowed, are still alive?"

"Run home quickly," she said to the seventh kid, "and bring my scissors and a needle and thread."

Then the mother goat cut open the wolf's stomach. At the first small cut she made, out popped the head of one little kid.

As she cut further along the wolf's stomach, more and more kids jumped out. Finally, all six of them were free and alive! Not one was hurt for, in his greed, the wolf had swallowed them whole.

How happy they all were to be together again.
The poor mother goat wept again, but this time
she wept for joy.

The seven little goats, in their happiness, skipped and jumped around the sleeping wolf.

Soon, however, the mother goat spoke to them. "Go and find some big stones," she said, "and bring them back to me."

So the seven little goats searched for the biggest stones they could find and took them to where the wolf lay.

The mother goat placed as many of the stones as she could inside the wolf's stomach. Then she quickly sewed it together again.

The wolf lay snoring the whole time and knew nothing of what had happened.

After a very long sleep, the wolf wakened and felt thirsty, so he set off for the well for a drink.

As he walked, the stones in his stomach knocked and rattled against each other. Then he cried out,

> "What rumbles and tumbles,
> Inside my poor bones?
> I ate six young kids
> But they feel like six stones."

It took him a long time to reach the well, swaying and rumbling as he went. When he got there, and bent over the water to drink, the heavy stones in his stomach made him topple over.

Head first into the well he fell, with a frightful plop.

49

The goat and her kids, hearing the frightful
plop, came running to the well. When they saw
that the wolf had drowned, great was their joy.

They skipped around crying, "The wolf is dead! The wolf is dead!" No longer did the mother goat need to be afraid to leave her kids alone when she went to the forest.